AGONDRAY

AGONDRAY

The Guardian of the Clouds

D.L. Goddard
Illustrated by: Donna Goddard, Ben Pepper, India Lawton

authorHOUSE®

AuthorHouse™
1663 Liberty Drive
Bloomington, IN 47403
www.authorhouse.com
Phone: 1-800-839-8640

Published by AuthorHouse   05/14/2012

ISBN: 978-1-4678-8516-4 (sc)
ISBN: 978-1-4678-8517-1 (e)

FOR PAPPY

"THE STORY TELLER"

CHAPTER 1

Are We There Yet?

It was the Easter holiday and Ella, Ben, and their dog, Jessie, were sitting in the car with Mum and Dad. They were on the way to visit their grandparents who lived on a farm in a small village called Cheriton.

"I'm bored," moaned Ella to her mum who was sitting in the passenger seat. "When are we going to be there?"

"Ella," said Mum firmly, "We only left the house five minutes ago. We are going to be quite a while. Why don't you and Ben play I spy?"

Ben looked up from his book. "Do I have to?"

"Would you mind, Ben? It will make the journey go quicker for both of you," replied Mum.

Ben and Ella got on quite well . . . most of the time. Ben, however, was four years older than his sister and, being thirteen, wanted to do his own thing.

You could tell they were brother and sister. They had very similar features: faces shaped the same with button noses. Both had dark hair. Ella's was long, just past her shoulders and Ben's was short and spiky. The only difference, really, was their eyes. Ben had blue eyes like his mum and Ella had brown eyes like her dad. And they did—despite what they would say—love each other very much.

After the children had been playing I spy for a while, Dad pulled the car over at a small road side café. They put the lead on Jessie and got out. Jessie sloped out of the back of the car and gave herself a good stretch and a big yawn.

When they got to the farm she would be able to have a good long run in one of the fields, chase dragon flies and poke her nose down rabbit holes. Jessie always liked going there; she could run around all day and make herself dizzy.

For now, she took a drink of water and then got back into the car while the others popped in to the café for a quick drink.

"Nearly there," said Dad while he sipped his coffee. "It's only about half an hour now."

"It's so boring; I want to be there now," said Ella. Ben nodded in agreement.

Ella was only nine years old and she hadn't quite mastered the concept of time. Ben tried to explain it to her, but she would say, "Is thirty minutes gone yet?" moments after someone told her, "We will be there in thirty minutes."

When they finished their drinks they paid the bill and got back in the car.

3

"Right, let's go," said Mum.

"I'm bored," said Ella as soon as the car pulled away.

"Okay," sighed Mum. "Let's try this. Look up into the sky and tell me what you see."

"Clouds and blue sky," said Ella grumpily.

"Try looking a bit harder. Can you see that dragon in the clouds? Look, there's a dog."

"Where? I can't see anything except clouds and sky."

Mum explained, "If you look at the shape of the clouds, sometimes you can see objects, animals, people, and shapes—but you have to have a bit of imagination."

Imagination was something Ella was not lacking (oh, how the fairies used to mess up her bedroom and throw all her clothes on the floor!). She sometimes used to pretend she was a teacher taking the register, a hair dresser with her own salon, or a restaurant owner, helping to lay the table—you would always have to make a booking with her before you could sit down to eat.

Ella looked up into the sky as her mum had suggested. As she did, she noticed something strange happening to the clouds—as if by magic they started to form shapes. Ella blinked in disbelief. It could not be possible.

"Mum," said Ella, "look up quick, the clouds are moving!"

"Yes, I know Ella," said her mum without looking up.

"No, look, the clouds are moving," Ella said with frustration. But her mum was too busy talking to her dad.

Ella sighed and turned to look back out of the window. She watched as the clouds seemed to almost dance across the beautiful, blue sky. She thought they looked like balls of cotton wool, soft and fluffy, scattered across the sky.

While she was looking up, she noticed the clouds moving again as they had done before. But she noticed one cloud that seemed to be moving in a different way across the sky. It wasn't just moving across; it seemed to be going up and down too. Ella looked carefully at the cloud, wondering what on earth it could be. Then, all of a sudden, the cloud just stopped. It seemed to turn around and, as it did, Ella gasped. She looked about to see if anyone had heard her, but no one had. Ben was too busy reading, and Mum and Dad too busy talking. What she saw looked just like a dragon.

Ella rubbed her eyes and looked back up into the sky. Still, the dragon shape was there.

It was looking straight at her. She wasn't scared because the dragon didn't look fierce. It looked very sad, and she couldn't help wondering why.

The dragon bowed its head to Ella and turned and carried on across the sky.

"Did I really see that?" thought Ella.

CHAPTER 2

The Farm

THE CAR CAME TO a stop and Ella looked around. Jessie started to get very excited, and Ben said, "We are here, Ella. Come on, let's get out."

Standing and waiting in the doorway were their grandparents, Robert and Ann, whom the children called Pappy and Nan. The children loved them very much because Pappy and Nan always spoiled them when they came to visit. There were always lots of nice things to do and eat and, best of all, exciting stories at bed time.

Pappy was the storyteller, telling stories of when he was at sea, fighting off a giant octopus from his fishing boat or punching a shark in the nose when he fell overboard and had to swim for days before anyone rescued him—he had to eat seaweed to ease his hunger.

The children rushed out of the car and ran up to their grandparents, throwing their arms around them excitedly.

Jessie went straight into the field next to the house and started running around and around. All the family started to laugh because, when she stopped, you could see her legs wobbling from dizziness. She stopped for a moment and then carried on again, around and around. Her head was bobbing up and down, and her great, long tongue was hanging out to one side. What a funny sight!

The house wasn't very big, but very pretty with baskets of flowers hanging by the door and in pots all along the front. It had two big windows on either side of the front door and three more above those and a chimney on the roof with smoke blowing out the top. Inside, it had a kitchen and lounge downstairs, two bedrooms and a bathroom on the next floor, and an attic room at the very top where the children would sleep.

They all went into the house and Nan had a pot of tea, some squash, and sandwiches laid out for them in the kitchen.

After they had eaten, the children took their things upstairs to their bedroom and unpacked.

Pappy called up to the children to see if they wanted to feed the animals. The children dashed down the stairs, put on their boots and coats, and went out to help.

They loved helping to look after the animals. Even Jessie would help by carrying a bucket of food. The farm was surrounded by beautiful countryside, and the nearest house seemed to be miles away. There were a couple of fields next to the house, a big barn at the back and an animal shed next to that, where all the animals were. There were a dozen or so chickens, four cows, and a few sheep with their lambs.

Once all the animals had been fed and watered the family went back inside. It was starting to get dark and a bit chilly.

Mum and Nan were preparing dinner, and Dad was trying his best to get the log fire burning in the lounge. The children took off their outdoor clothes and washed their hands. Jessie had her dinner and a drink and then went to lie down in front of the fire.

The children laid the table, and Ella, of course, took bookings for that evening and checked with Nan to see if they had a table that could seat six.

Once they had laid the table, they went to sit in the lounge with Dad and Pappy.

"How was the journey?" asked Pappy.

"Boring," replied Ella, "but something happened when we got back in the car after we had stopped for a drink."

"What was that, Ella?" asked Pappy.

"Well, you know how if you look up into the sky you find shapes and things? I saw something very strange . . . a dragon."

"That's only because Mum told you there was a dragon in the clouds. But she only meant the shape of the cloud looked a bit like a dragon," said Ben.

"No, that's not it. The cloud was definitely a dragon; a cloud dragon."

Ben scoffed at his sister and walked back into the kitchen. Dad followed him and told him not to forget how much younger his sister was. Then he reminded Ben that he used to have an invisible friend.

"You believe me, Pappy, don't you?"

"I believe you," said Pappy. "Come on, let's go into the kitchen. I can hear your mum calling. We'll talk more at bedtime."

They all sat down and enjoyed their meal. It was a nice, big roast chicken with lots of vegetables and lashings of gravy—the children's favourite (and Nan made the best gravy in the world).

Once they had finished, the children helped clear the table and they all went into the lounge to play some games. When they went to visit their grandparents they didn't watch television or play computer games. There were plenty of other things to do, such as helping with the animals, going for walks with Jessie through the fields, and helping to get the meals ready. In the evenings they would play charades and snap. Ben and Pappy had been playing the same game of chess for the past two years, and neither was any closer to winning.

At nine o'clock, Mum told the children it was time for bed. They kissed Mum, Dad, and Nan goodnight, and Pappy said he would be up once they had brushed their teeth and gotten into bed.

The children raced up the stairs as they were looking forward to Pappy's story, wondering what it could be about this time.

Little did they know that tonight's story was to be the most exciting of all!

CHAPTER 3

An Unbelievable Story!

BEN AND ELLA QUICKLY brushed their teeth and got into bed. The room was right under the roof of the house, but it was lovely and cosy thanks to the big, thick quilts on the beds and lots of cushions. It had beams on the ceiling, a small wardrobe and a dresser with a mirror on top next to the window.

The grown-ups had to duck their heads when they came in through the door.

Pappy came up and sat at the end of Ella's bed. "What's the story about tonight?" asked Ella. "Snuggle down in bed and I'll begin." Both the children lay down and pulled the covers around them.

"Ella," Pappy said, "The dragon you saw, what did it look like?"

"Oh, no," groaned Ben.

"Why?" asked Ella.

"Just tell me," said Pappy with a smile.

"Well," Ella began, "it looked like a cloud. Oh, and it seemed sad," she said softly.

"What else can you tell me?" asked Pappy.

"It bowed its head at me and then carried on across the sky. I wasn't scared," she said.

"What is it Pappy," asked Ben, "what do you know?"

Pappy turned to Ella. He had a worried look on his face. "One more question, Ella, did it have anything around its neck?"

"No, I don't think so. Why?" asked Ella.

"I had hoped this day would never come."

Ben looked up, his face full of questions. But, at the same time, he was trying not to look interested because he thought it might just be one of Pappy's stories.

"What did you say, Pappy? What do you mean?"

"The amulet is missing," said Pappy.

"What's that?" asked Ben impatiently, still trying to seem disinterested.

"Agondray's amulet. The dragon you saw is called Agondray. I know it was him because he bowed to you. The other dragons would not have done that."

"Other dragons?" asked Ben and Ella together.

"I'll tell you the story," said Pappy.

"Agondray was the guardian of the clouds. He was the biggest, bravest and most respected dragon next to King Razil.

The king and his wife, Queen Zeya, ruled over the whole of Cloud Land from the main city, called Gibiuss.

It was the most beautiful city you have ever seen. An incredible castle stood in the centre of the city. The rooftops glistened like crystals and went high up into the blue sky. The castle itself looked like it was made from precious stones: diamonds, rubies and emeralds all shimmering in the sun.

The castle was surrounded by lots of houses where all the dragons of Gibiuss lived.

They were friendly dragons and would do anything to help a friend or neighbour. It was a very peaceful city.

"One day a dragon called Zell went to Gibiuss and sent waves of fear and panic throughout the city.

Zell was the most dangerous dragon in the whole of Cloud Land. He was even feared in his home city, called Neptur, which was where some of the most wicked and evil dragons lived.

Neptur was a very dark city with many of the buildings destroyed by fire and fighting.

The dragons there would think nothing of destroying their neighbours' house or stealing from them. The dragons of Neptur were not supposed to leave their own city, but Zell wanted to rule the whole of Cloud Land and had come to destroy the kingdom and take over as king. But he knew that to take over, he would have to get rid of Agondray first.

"A great battle between Agondray and Zell took place. There were huge waves of fire and roars so loud the clouds shook beneath their feet. I remember we had quite a storm here that night. The sky lit up like fireworks, and the noise was deafening. The animals were very scared, and Nan and I ended up spending the night in the barn with them. Of course, at the time, we didn't know what was going on.

The fierce battle continued for several days until, quite suddenly, Zell stopped, exhausted and badly hurt. He told Agondray that he knew he could not defeat him and knelt down in front of him, prepared to die. Agondray told Zell he would not kill him but demanded that he leave, and, if he ever returned, he would not be allowed to live.

"Great celebrations followed and lasted for many days. King Razil presented Agondray with an amulet in honour of his bravery in protecting the kingdom.

An amulet is a charm that, some say, offers protection and healing powers to the one who wears it. Up until today, there has been peace."

The children sat there in silence and then suddenly Ben started to laugh.

"Good one, Pap! You really had me going then!"

Pappy sat there quietly for a moment and sighed deeply, "I wish I was joking Ben. I know it is a lot to take in and sounds like one of my stories, but I'm afraid this one is true."

"But how could you know all this?" Ben asked.

"When I was a boy, during the war, my friends and I used to play in all sorts of places. Bombed houses, timber yards, and anywhere else we were not supposed to go. We had a great time exploring. We would build ourselves dens and sit around, chatting and cooking scraps, that we'd been given by the butcher, in metal tins.

We had one particular den in a wooded area, up a slight hill. We used to go there on Saturdays, climb up in the trees, and just spend the day messing about. We'd have a lot of fun."

Pappy paused. What he was about to tell them would change everything forever.

"One Saturday, my friends had been naughty so none of them were allowed out. I decided to go to the den up the hill on my own.

I had been up a tree for quite a while and was starting to get a bit bored, so I decided to go home. As I climbed down, out of the corner of my eye, I saw something move. I thought maybe it was a fox or a badger or something, so I ignored it and kept climbing down.

I then heard a noise and turned to see where it was coming from. As I got closer, I could see something trying to hide behind a tree—not very well, I might add, because it was large. It was a funny-looking, misty sort of object. Of course, being curious, I got closer to have a look.

"To my absolute amazement, it appeared to be a dragon! Although I'd seen pictures of them in my schoolbooks, as far as I knew dragons didn't exist. But there was no mistake that this was definitely a dragon. It didn't look like the ones I'd seen in the books; it was a sort of white, grey colour. It actually looked like a cloud, and I reached out to touch it.

The dragon moved away from me slightly and then, realising I wasn't a threat, moved towards me and allowed me to stroke him. As he did, the misty appearance vanished and there stood an enormous, strong, red and green dragon.

"When the cloud dragons first come into contact with humans, they try to disguise themselves with the cloud mist. They only reveal themselves once they are sure there is no threat."

Pappy continued on, "He rubbed his head against me and knocked me over; he was very strong.

And then he spoke. 'My name is Agondray and I need your help.' I remember I fell over again in shock. Did it really just talk to me? It's not every day you meet a dragon, let alone one that can speak!

"He turned his head towards his wing, and I noticed he had hurt it. I moved back towards him to look at his wing. He explained that he had been flying through the sky when something—a funny, noisy object that we humans call a plane—hit him and knocked him out of the sky. He had landed badly in the woods, damaging his wing. (I heard a few days later that an enemy plane had crash landed, but they didn't know why . . . just that it had a huge dent on the side that didn't match the crash damage.)

"Over the next few weeks, I went up to the woods whenever I could to nurse Agondray back to health. He would tell me stories of his home, about the castle, his neighbours, the king and queen and, of course, he told me about Zell.

"Eventually he was strong enough to return home. He thanked me for caring for him and asked if there was anything he could do for me. I told him there wasn't—only that it would be nice for my new friend to visit from time to time. He promised he would and then flew high up into the sky, vanishing from sight.

"He kept his promise and visited whenever he could. Sometimes he would take me on his back and fly over the town. No one could see us, of course, because, from below, he looked like a cloud.

He has been a part of my life and your Nan's ever since. He would visit us if he thought it was safe to do so, sometimes late at night. He visited us just after the battle with Zell. He wanted to show us his amulet. We were so proud of him.

"To be honest, we haven't really seen him since—only a quick pass over in the sky, and now it seems there is a reason. Something is very wrong in Cloud Land . . . so wrong he hasn't even been able to come and see us because he feels it's not safe for us or him.

The fact that the amulet is gone is a sure sign of trouble. He must have been looking for me when you saw him."

"Why, Pappy?" asked the children together.

"Because I am the only human he trusts," replied Pappy.

The children sat there, mouths wide open, in total shock at what their grandfather had just told them.

"In the morning, we must go up to Slippery Hill. Agondray will meet us there and, perhaps, we can find out what has happened. Go to sleep now. We have a very important day ahead of us. Oh, and don't say anything to your parents; this must be our secret and, besides, they would only think it was one of my stories."

Pappy kissed the children goodnight and turned out the light.

"There's no way I'm going to be able to sleep now," said Ben. "Me either," said Ella.

"I can't believe Pappy is friends with a cloud dragon. Ben, this is so exciting! What do you think will happen tomorrow?" Ben mumbled something to his sister and Ella realised he had fallen asleep.

"I'm too excited to sleep" Ella said to herself, "but I had better try."

Sure enough, Ella was soon sleeping soundly too.

Pappy went down stairs and rejoined the rest of the family in the lounge. "You must have been telling them an epic tale this time," said Nan. "I was," replied Pappy. He smiled at his wife.

The grown-ups chatted for a while, and then Mum said she was tired and would see them in the morning. She and Dad went up to bed.

"What's going on?" asked Nan once they were alone.

Pappy explained everything and Nan listened carefully.

"Right," Nan said. "We will go and see Agondray in the morning. We will tell their parents we are going to take the children out for the day so they can have a break, and I will pack a lunch for us all."

Nan then started going up to bed herself. "Come on, you need to rest. Tomorrow could be very busy," she said.

"Okay," Pappy replied. "I'm coming."

Pappy got up and walked over to the large, oak dresser in the lounge and opened the drawer. In it was a small blue pouch. He took it out and put it in his pocket and then went on up to bed.

CHAPTER 4

The Meeting

THE CHILDREN WOKE UP early, quietly got dressed, brushed their teeth and hair and crept down stairs to find Pappy and Nan busy in the kitchen.

"Sit down children; I will fix you some breakfast. We have got a long day ahead of us; you will need all your strength," Nan said.

The children looked at each other and then at Pappy. "Agondray will be waiting for us. He needs our help, so you mustn't be afraid."

"I'm just going to tell your parents we are taking you out for the day for a picnic. Eat up and then we will go," said Nan. She went up stairs to speak to the grown-ups.

Once they were ready, the four of them set off towards Slippery Hill with Pappy taking the lead. They walked along a lane for what seemed like miles. There were tall trees and bushes on either side. Every now and then there was a gate, and Ella would stop and have a look at the animals in the field. They walked past Pappy and Nan's neighbour, who was in his front garden and they all said good morning and carried on walking. Eventually they came to a big wooden gate that looked like it was in need of repair. Some of the slats were broken off altogether and others were badly cracked. Pappy carefully opened the gate and they all walked through and into a field. He pointed to a hill in front of them and told them it was Slippery Hill. "Not too long now, children," said Nan. They walked on, not really saying anything to each other. All of them felt a little nervous about what lay ahead.

Once they reached the bottom of the hill Pappy stopped, turned to the children, and said,

"Okay, we are going to go up the hill to the line of trees you can see at the top, and I will call Agondray. You mustn't be afraid; he won't hurt you."

When they reached the line of trees, the children looked around. They could see for miles, they could even see the farm. But once they went in to the thick of the trees, it was hard to see anything. They could see why Agondray would hide there. It seemed quite safe for someone or something that did not want to be seen.

"He will be here soon, children, so remember what I said," Pappy said as he pulled the blue pouch out of his pocket. He opened the pouch and pulled out a necklace with a stone on the end. He placed it around his neck and it started to glow.

"Oh," said Ella. "It's beautiful. What is it?"

"Years ago, Agondray gave this to me as a thank you for caring for him. He said to bring it here and put it on if I ever needed him. I think it will work the same now that he needs us," explained Pappy.

They stood in silence, the children feeling very nervous and quite scared.

Suddenly there was a whooshing sound and then nothing.

"Hello, Agondray," said Pappy.

"Hello, Robert, my old friend," said a voice from behind a tree.

Ben and Ella looked, desperately trying to see who or what was speaking, but all they could see was a mist behind one of the huge tree trunks.

Eventually, they saw some movement behind the tree, and then an enormous head appeared . . . followed by an enormous body and tail. It was Agondray.

He was absolutely amazing—even more spectacular than Pappy's description. When he stood up, his head almost reached as high as some of the tree tops. His huge chest was a blazing red, and the rest of his body was the darkest green. He slowly lowered his head so he could see the children as they stood with their mouths open, totally shocked. His golden eyes sparkled as he spoke.

"It's rude to stare," he said, and the children staggered backwards.

"S-s-sorry," the children stammered.

"That's okay," Agondray said and began to chuckle.

He turned to Pappy and Nan and said, "Friends it's good to see you both again. I'm just sorry these are not happier times."

"It's good to see you too," said Pappy, "These are my grandchildren, Ben and Ella. Children, say hello to Agondray."

"H-h-hello," they both stuttered.

"Thank you Ella for telling your grandfather you had seen me. I knew who you were when I saw you because I've seen photographs of you both on my many visits. Plus, I knew your family liked to visit during this time of year. I thought I would take my chances with letting you see me because it was not safe for me to go to your grandfather's house at the moment."

"Agondray, where is your amulet?" asked Pappy.

Agondray lowered his head. "Zell has returned," he said, pausing before continuing with his story.

"One night he returned, taking us all by surprise. He managed to capture the king and queen and is holding them in the castle prison. The city has been destroyed by Zell's followers. Some of my fellow dragons have been killed, but many more have managed to escape and are hiding in caves. Even I was captured by Zell. He took my amulet and told me to leave Gibiuss. I was ashamed that I could not protect the city and this pleased Zell. But, because I had let him live, he offered me the same courtesy. But then he warned that if I ever went near the outskirts of the city he would know and kill the king and queen. It is not my life I am worried about; it is theirs. I feel so ashamed for allowing this to happen."

Pappy walked up to Agondray reached up, and put his hand on his shoulder. "You mustn't feel ashamed; there was nothing you could have done. We now need to focus on how to put things right. Sit down, everyone. We need to come up with a plan."

They all sat down and Nan got out some drinks and sandwiches. They started talking about how to get to Cloud Land and, once there, what they would do, where they would go first, and who they could trust.

Agondray told them there was one dragon he could trust and knew where she was hiding. Her name was Akoya. She had been the queen's advisor and confidante and a very good friend of his. He trusted her with his life.

It was agreed that they would meet the next day and go to Cloud Land to find Akoya. That would give them time to pack some essentials. Pappy would arrange for his neighbour to look after the animals until they got back. He would tell him they were going camping for a few days—he also had to think of a way to get the children away from their parents.

Agondray bowed to his friends and flew up into the air and, with a whoosh, was gone.

"You don't have to come," said Pappy as they walked home.

"You are joking, aren't you Pappy? Do you really think Ella and I could stay at home with all this going on and, besides, you need all the help you can get. We will be fine," Ben said.

"I know we need your help; I am just worried that it could be dangerous. Your parents would never forgive me if anything happened," Pappy replied.

"We will be fine. Don't forget we have the bravest dragon on our side," insisted Ella as they made their way home.

As they got close to the farm, Mum came out to meet them. Jessie bounded out the door and ran up to the children.

"I'm glad you're home. Have you had a good day?" asked Mum.

"We've had the best time, Mum," said Ella.

"That's great; but I'm afraid I have some bad news, we have to return home. Dad had a phone call from work, and there is a serious problem. I'm so sorry, but we have to go."

"Oh, no! We've only just got here!" cried Ella.

"I know, Ella. I am sorry, but we need to leave as soon as we can."

Both the children started to moan and pleaded with their mum to let them stay.

"The children can stay with us. You can pick them up at the end of the week if that would help. It would be nice to spend some time with them, and you can sort out your problem without the worry of these two," Nan said.

"Oh, yes-yes," said Ella. "Please, can we stay?"

"Well, if you're sure," said Dad as he appeared at the front door. "It would be a big help, and we will be back on Friday. We will take Jessie to keep Mum company while I'm working and bring her back too. I'm afraid we need to leave now. We had better go and pack," he said.

Pappy turned to the children quietly saying, "What a stroke of luck. We'll see them off and then get ourselves sorted."

That night, Pappy and Nan organised the things they needed to take: torches, rope, bottles of water, sandwiches, and a few other things. The children had gone to bed early—the excitement had totally worn them out.

"They are in for quite an adventure," Nan said to Pappy as they walked up to bed.

"Yes, I know. I just hope we can help Agondray."

CHAPTER 5

Up into the Clouds

THE NEXT MORNING EVERYONE was up early. In fact, the sun hadn't even risen yet.

It had been arranged for Agondray to meet them behind the farm's barn. As it was early, it would be quite safe, and now the children's parents were gone—even better.

Nan had made some breakfast for them. "Eat up," she said, "you'll need your energy." The children sat down and ate their breakfast as fast as they could.

Just as they had finished and were putting the bowls away they heard a whooshing sound and then nothing.

"He's here," Pappy said. "Come on, then. Let's go."

Ben and Ella grabbed their coats and backpacks and raced out through the back door, absolutely bursting with excitement. Pappy and Nan followed behind the children. They locked the house and made their way to the back of the barn.

Agondray was waiting for them. "Good morning, Agondray," said the children together, still not quite believing they were about to get on a dragons back and go to another world. "Good morning," said Agondray. "Let me crouch down so you can climb on." He lowered his wing for them to step on and then gently lifted it so they could climb on his back.

Pappy had managed to tie a huge rope around Agondray's neck to give him something to hold onto. Ella put her arms around Pappy, Ben held onto his sister and Nan sat at the back, holding onto Ben.

"Okay, Agondray, we are ready. Hold on tight, everyone." Pappy said.

With that, Agondray opened his enormous wings and started to flap. Both the children shut their eyes and held on tightly to the person in front of them. They could feel a breeze from the flapping of his wings and then suddenly felt the wind blasting into their faces as they flew up into the sky. Ben opened one eye to take a peek and then quickly shut it again.

When the children did eventually open their eyes, they could see the land below them getting smaller and smaller and then, all of a sudden, they were up in the clouds and the land was gone, out of sight. Agondray was racing along, getting faster and faster with every flap of his giant wings.

They flew for miles and miles. Until, in the distance, they noticed a strange group of clouds. As they got closer they realised it was five roughly shaped circles overlapping one another with what seemed to be a small gap in the middle.

As they approached, the circles started to move and the gap appeared to open up, making enough room for them to fly through. As they did, Agondray slowed down and, in the distance, they could see something—it looked like another world.

"How did that happen?" asked Ben.

Agondray laughed and said, "You would never know we were here."

He flew on for a little bit longer and then started to go down towards Cloud Land.

They could see lots of mountains with trees dotting the sides and tops. They glistened with snow. In the distance there appeared to be black smoke rising up into the sky. "That is where the castle is," Agondray said to them.

He slowed down some more and started to go down towards a clearing in between some mountains. As they got lower they could see movement on the ground and then realised it was dragons, lots of them.

The children started to get scared and Agondray could sense it. "Don't be afraid; they are my friends. They won't hurt you," he reassured them. The children relaxed a little but were still nervous and wondered what the day would bring.

Agondray landed softly and crouched down so they could climb off. "Welcome to my home. This is Dew Mountain," Agondray said. "Wow, it's so beautiful!" said Ella.

As they brushed themselves down and took off their backpacks, Ben noticed a dragon—a little smaller than Agondray—walking towards them. He grabbed his sister and they stood close to their grandparents. "Agondray, I am so glad to see you are safe. There is so much to talk about . . . who are the humans?" asked the dragon.

"Akoya, I would like you to meet my friends," said Agondray. "Do you remember the story I told you? When I got knocked out of the sky and a human saved me? Well, this is Robert, his wife, Ann, and these are his grandchildren, Ben and Ella."

Akoya bowed her head slightly, "I am honoured to meet you all. Agondray has spoken many times of you, and I am so pleased to meet you at last. But I am afraid it is not safe to stay out in the open; we must move into the cover of the cave," she said, pointing in the direction of a big cave on the side of the mountain.

She was very pretty: her eyes were the brightest green, her face and chest were a pale pink and the rest of her was a beautiful lilac colour.

"What has happened since I have been gone?" asked Agondray as they made their way to the cave. "Not much has changed. The king and queen are still locked up in the castle, and Zell and his followers are destroying everything in their path," Akoya said, tears welling up in her eyes as she spoke. "We don't know what to do, Agondray. Everyone is so scared."

"That is why Robert said he would help. They can get into the castle without being noticed. We have a plan, but everyone will need to help. We know it will work," said Agondray.

"How do you know?" Akoya asked. Agondray turned to face her. "Because it has to," he replied, smiling.

That night they talked through the plan that Pappy and Agondray had come up with. All of the other dragons listened. Agondray asked if some of his dragon friends would be willing to fight with them. "I don't want you to say yes now; I would like you to think about it—it will be dangerous. Please just step forward before we leave at first light," said Agondray.

The children already knew what they had to do and felt very excited but also a bit scared. Would Pappy's plan work . . . without any one getting hurt?

But, as Agondray, had said: it had to.

CHAPTER 6

Ben and Ella's Big Rescue

JUST BEFORE THE SUN came up Pappy woke the children. "Wake up; it's time to go. Nan has made you some breakfast; come and eat while we go over the final details," said Pappy.

They got out of their makeshift beds of moss-type stuff and straw and went to see Nan, who was busy with the food. They sat down and listened as Pappy, Agondray and Akoya went over the last details of the plan.

A very large group of dragons gathered close to the meeting spot and one stepped forward and spoke, "We would like to volunteer, Agondray."

"Thank you for your bravery, you are true friends," replied Agondray. "Split yourselves into two groups: one will follow Akoya and the rest will come with me. We will be ready to leave soon." Agondray then turned to the children and asked, "How are you feeling this morning?"

"A little scared to be honest," said Ben. Ella nodded her head in agreement.

"Everything will be fine. You and Ella are not in any danger. Your job is the easy one; our job is the difficult one. And I know you will not let us down. Besides, your grand parents will be with you all the way," Agondray said.

Once everyone had eaten and bags had been packed again they stood in a circle and Agondray said a few words, "Friends, today is the day we take back our land and rid Gibiuss of Zell once and for all. The road we take is not an easy one, but as long as we work together, protect each other and focus on the task, we will all stay safe. The humans must stay safe. This is not their fight, yet they are here to help. Not only that, you all know how our battles affect the world below us, causing terrible thunder storms. We must finish this as quickly as possible to keep any damage to earth to an absolute minimum.

"Robert has a flare, which is a bright light that he will shoot up in to the sky once the king and queen are safe. When you see that, it is time. You each know your role; stick to that. Only do the job you have been asked to do. Keep safe and we will all meet when this is over. Robert, Akoya, it is time for us to go."

With that, all the other dragons flew off to wait—not too far from the city, but far enough not to be seen.

"We must leave now. Robert and Ben, you will come with me. Ella and Ann, go with Akoya. We will meet at the hill just behind the castle. We must be silent and quick because we need to fly over part of the city. Speed is the key, so hold on tight," said Agondray.

They climbed onto the dragons and, before they knew it, they were up in the sky and heading towards the castle as fast as they could go. As they approached the city the children looked down and could see buildings still burning. Many had been totally destroyed with only ash remaining. The ground was scorched from the flames, and they could see dragons lying on the ground, sleeping.

Both dragons flew silently down to the ground and landed behind a hill, out of sight of the castle. Everyone got off the dragons and prepared to go.

In the distance the low drone of dragons sleeping could be heard. Ella looked at Ben and held his hand tightly. "It's okay, Ella. Stick close to me; I'll look after you," said Ben reassuringly.

"We must leave you here," said Agondray. "Akoya and I must meet with our fellow dragons to prepare for the attack. We will wait for your signal."

"Keep safe," Akoya said, "We will see you once this is over. Remember to get back to Dew Mountain as soon as you can and stay there until we come for you."

"Good luck," said Agondray and, with that, he and Akoya left.

"Well, it's down to us now," whispered Pappy. "We must make our way around the hill on this path to the back of the castle. It is important that we are as quiet as possible, and we must not speak. When we get there you know what you must do. But remember, Nan and I are here, you will be safe. It is most important that we free the king and queen before the battle starts. Good luck, children. We are very proud of you."

They set off in silence and started on the path around the hill. It wasn't too long before they could see the castle on the other side. Ella nearly gasped at the beauty of it but clasped her hand over her mouth just in time.

It was totally amazing and just how Pappy had described it. It was huge, bigger than any building she had ever seen. As they got closer they struggled to see the tops of the towers reaching high up into the sky. The doors on the castle were enormous—as big as two or three buses stacked on top of each other—and the windows were as big as cars. The whole building shimmered in the sun despite having some fire damage to it.

As they reached the back of the castle they kept low and very quiet. There was a smallish window low to the ground, which Ben thought was very odd compared to the size of everything else. But Agondray had already explained that this window was only there to put a little bit of light into the castle prison. Obviously, its size meant a dragon could not escape; but, luckily for them, a human child could get in.

Pappy quietly took off his backpack and the others did the same. He knelt down in front of the window and pulled out a metal bar from his bag. He slid the bar between the gap at the bottom of the window and managed to slide the catch along on the inside. Nan held a suction cup that stuck onto the window and slowly pulled it towards them while Pappy very carefully pulled the bar back. He turned and nodded at the children and smiled. The children had been busy tying ropes around their waists so they would be ready to be lowered into the dungeon. Nan held the window open as far as she could, and Ben and Ella crouched down by the opening. Pappy then carefully lowered them in, first Ben and then Ella. Once the children were in safely, Pappy and Nan blew them both a kiss and closed the window. Now all they could do was go back and hide behind the hill and wait.

Once the children were inside they untied the ropes and stood still for a moment to let their eyes adjust to the poor light in the dungeon. It was very dark, but they could just make out what appeared to be extremely thick bars on either side of them. Ben had a torch in his pocket, which he got out and turned on. They looked around and could see that the thick bars were, in fact, parts of prison cells. There were huge chains on the floors within the cells. As he shone the torch around, they heard a noise. Ella grabbed onto her brother, shaking. "Who's there?" said a very soft, weak voice. Ben shone the torch in that direction and could just make out a couple of large shapes on the far side of another cell.

"Are you Queen Zeya?" Ben said in the quietest voice he could, trying not to sound scared.

"Yes, I am," said the queen, and the children saw one of the shapes slowly move towards them. "Our names are Ben and Ella. We are friends of Agondray and we have come to get you out," said Ben.

"Is that the king with you?" said Ella in her bravest voice. "Yes, it is the king. But he was hurt in the fighting and is very weak—we both are. I don't know if we are strong enough to escape," said the queen.

"You must try. We have to get you out of here now. Agondray is waiting for our signal, ready to attack and take back the castle," said Ben anxiously.

"Akoya gave us some things that may help," Ella added.

"Very well," said the queen, "We will try."

And with that she disappeared into the shadows.

Moments later she reappeared with the king at her side, he looked very tired and frail. Both of the dragons appeared grey in colour, with a slight mist around them. Their heads were hanging down, and they were obviously too weak to try to escape without help.

Ella noticed his wing was badly damaged and he had big cuts on his side and head. She had been given some special ointment by Akoya, who told her to rub it in to any wounds the king or queen might have.

Ben had also been given a tonic to give to the king and queen. This would give them the energy and strength they needed to escape.

As the children treated the king and queen they saw their colour change and the mist disappear. The king suddenly appeared much larger with a deep red chest and an emerald-green body. The queen was the most vibrant purple with a bronze chest. Both had bright, sparkling, yellow eyes.

The king turned to the children and said, "Thank you, Ben and Ella." He then bowed his head, saying, "Please let me introduce myself. I am Razil and this is Zeya. We are both feeling much better now. I have been too weak to attempt to leave, so we have had to wait to be rescued—although we did not expect to see humans coming to rescue us!" He paused and bowed his head again and spoke, "We will be forever in your debt. There is a secret passage near the window where you came in; we just need to get out of this cell. Please move away from the bars." As they did, the king blew a ribbon of fire from his mouth. It seemed to wrap itself around the bars and they started to melt—the heat was unbearable. The children shielded their eyes and moved farther away. The fire disappeared and, as they looked up, they saw that the king and queen were right next to them. "The passage will bring us out past the hill at the back of the castle. Agondray is the only one who knows about this besides us. Unfortunately, it can only be used to get out, not in. Before, we were too weak to escape our cell; it was useless for us to even try."

The king pushed a stone into the wall, just to the side of the small window they had used to get in. As he did that, there was a loud scraping noise and a door opened before them. "We must be quick; I'm sure we have been heard," the king said.

It was very dark and the children could not see. Ben shone his torch down the long passage and grabbed hold of his sister's hand. "Stay close to me," he whispered to her. The queen moved into the passage first and told the children they could hold on to her tail and she would guide them through. The king followed behind and made sure the secret door closed behind them.

They walked quickly and quietly through the passage, and Ella held on tightly to her brother. The passage was dark and damp with little streams of water coming down the walls in places.

Ella thought she heard a noise and jumped. "It's okay," said Ben. Ella held on to him even more tightly. The passage seemed to go on forever until the queen suddenly stopped. She pulled another lever and a door opened into bright daylight. The children had to shield their eyes as they walked outside and, as they did, Nan and Pappy rushed to greet them.

"We are so proud of you. Well done!" said Nan, hugging both of the children.

Pappy approached the king and queen saying, "I am glad to see you are both safe and well. We are Robert and Ann, the children's grandparents, friends of Agondray. He has asked us to get you away from here as quickly as possible because it is not safe for us to stay. Can you fly and carry us?"

"Yes, thanks to Ben and Ella. You must be very proud of them," replied the king.

"Yes, we are. Thank you," said pappy, "We need to go to the clearing at Dew Mountain. It is not too far for you to fly, and we can tell you what is happening once we get there." Pappy then turned to Ben and Ella, "The queen will take you both, and we will fly with the king. We must get going." The children climbed onto the queens back and Pappy and Nan got onto the king's back. As soon as everyone was ready, Pappy took out the flare and said, "When I let off the flare, you must fly as fast as you can; the rest is up to Agondray now."

"Very well," replied the king.

With that, Pappy let off the flare and, before he could say anything, both dragons were up in the sky, flying as fast as they could towards Dew Mountain.

CHAPTER 7

The Battle to Take Back the Castle

IN THE DISTANCE, AGONDRAY saw the flare shoot high up into the sky and he turned and spoke to Akoya, "Keep safe." She looked at him with a tear in her eye. "It will be fine, as long as we stick to the plan," he reassured her. "I know. I'm just a little afraid . . . you might get hurt. That Zell . . ." Akoya couldn't quite get the words out. "I will be fine, he won't win this time," Agondray said and moved towards Akoya, brushing her neck with his nose. She looked at him and smiled and, without saying another word, they both took to the sky and the other dragons followed closely behind.

As they approached the castle they could hear loud roars and shouting. Agondray assumed the king and queen's escape had been discovered and knew he had to be quick to take them by surprise. Zell would be unprepared for an attack. They flew faster and faster and, as they approached the city, they split off into two groups, Akoya leading one and Agondray the other. They threw fire out of their mouths as they went, aiming the streams of flames at anything that moved. They took all of Zell's followers by surprise and caused confusion and chaos.

When Zell's followers realised what was happening and saw how many dragons were coming down from the sky, they started to panic. Some decided to flee, afraid of being captured or worse.

A few braver ones tried to fight back, shooting fire from their mouths and trying to bring the dragons down. Agondray's dragons flew on, charging at the dragons on the ground and throwing fireballs at them until those dragons, some injured retreated back to Neptur. Soon, only the dragons guarding the castle were left.

Agondray and his dragons flew down to the ground and made sure the city outside the castle was safe and free from Zell's followers.

Agondray looked around at what was left of a city that was once beautiful and peaceful. It had been almost totally destroyed. A few buildings were still burning, and there were piles of ash on the ground where some dragon's homes used to be. It would take time to rebuild the city, but they would. Akoya and her group landed next to Agondray and they all looked around in total dismay at what was once their home.

Agondray turned to his friends and said, "Our city has been all but destroyed, but our fighting spirit hasn't. Do not be down hearted at what you see. We can, in time, rebuild our city, but we must fight on and take back the castle. Akoya, you and your group must stay here to protect the city in case Zell's dragons come back. My group must move fast. Zell now knows we are here, and this time they will be ready for us." Once again, he took to the sky and his friends followed.

As they flew over the castle wall they could see Zell's followers in the court yard and a stronger guard in front of the entrance to the great hall. Agondray knew that was where Zell was.

They swooped down into the castle, weaving in between the towers and pillars and sending huge balls of fire at Zell's followers. One of Agondray's friends got knocked out of the sky by a ball of flames from below and landed with a crash in the courtyard. Agondray turned to see if he was okay and saw his friend get up, shake his head and then promptly fall back down again. At least he appeared to be only slightly hurt.

The rest of Agondray's friends carried on and cleared the way for him. Fire and smoke filled the entrance to the great hall, and cries could be heard as they fought. It was a nasty fight; dragons from both sides had been hurt but, eventually, Agondray's group proved too strong and overpowered Zell's guards until they surrendered and bowed down.

"Stay here and guard the prisoners," Agondray said to the rest of his group. "I will deal with Zell." With that, he burst through the doors and found Zell waiting for him.

"Did you really think I would leave and let you take over Cloud Land without a fight?" Agondray shouted.

"I did wonder how long it would take you to come back. Shame that this time I must kill you."

Zell roared at Agondray and the walls around them shook. He charged, smashing into Agondray and wounding his neck and knocking him off his feet. The glass in the windows shattered as Agondray hit the floor and shook the building.

Zell shouted at Agondray, "This is going to be too easy. One knock and you go down like a deck of cards. You were foolish to come back. Once you are dead, my followers will return and kill your friends, the king and that pretty one—Akoya, isn't it?"

Agondray felt the anger rise inside him. Zell would not beat him this time, he must protect the kingdom, his friends and, of course, Akoya. Somehow he found the strength to get to his feet.

"No, Zell, you are wrong. It is you who will die." And with that, Agondray charged at Zell with all his might, roaring the loudest roar and breathing the hottest fire he could summon. He struck Zell with the force of a high-speed train, sending him to the ground.

Zell sat there for a moment, stunned by the sudden force of Agondray. He should have known he was no match for the guardian of the clouds. "I warned you last time that if you returned I would kill you," Agondray roared as he walked towards Zell. Zell looked at Agondray and tried to get up but he couldn't—it was only then he realised how badly he had been hurt. Agondray looked at Zell and noticed he was wearing his amulet. He leaned towards Zell and took it from his neck, saying, "You had no right to come here, and you had no right to take this. Did you think it would protect you from me?" Agondray then put the amulet back around his own neck, and the stone gleamed like it knew it was back with its rightful owner.

Agondray knew that Zell was no longer a threat, so he turned his back on him. As he did, Zell blew out a small puff of smoke and was gone. Agondray walked out to the castle's courtyard where the dragons, including Akoya, were waiting for him. "Where are the prisoners?" he asked. "They are being guarded in the rear courtyard," one of the dragons said.

"Bring them to me" said Agondray.

Agondray's dragons ushered Zell's followers to him and then spoke to them all. "Your leader has gone," Agondray announced, and a cheer broke out from his friends and also from some of Zell's followers. "I am not going to lock you up in our prison as you did to our king and queen, although I should. I am going to give you the chance to leave, but you must never return to Gibiuss. However, I would like to offer you the chance to stay here among friendly dragons. We are going to need all the help we can get to rebuild the city and, as long as you prove yourself to be hard working, good hearted and able to live in peace in our city, you will be granted permission to stay for the rest of your lives. But you will not be allowed back into your old city; you must cut off all contact."

The dragons spoke among themselves for a short while, and then one stepped forward. "We would very much like to stay. Agondray, we know that we do not deserve this opportunity, but we are very humbled by it and will do whatever it takes to prove we deserve to stay here."

"Thank you," said Agondray. He turned to all his friends, including his new ones and said, "You will all rest today, but the hard work will start in the morning."

Akoya walked up to Agondray and said, "You're hurt." "It's nothing," he replied and, as he spoke, the amulet began to glow and his wounds began to heal.

"Akoya, Zell is dead and the war is over. Send your group out to spread the word, and tell everyone it is safe to return. My group will stay here to look after our new friends," Agondray said as he nodded in the direction of the prisoners. "We must go to Dew Mountain and tell the king and queen. They will be pleased to come home. It is also time Robert and his family returned to earth."

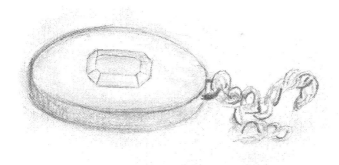

CHAPTER 8

Time to Go Home

B EN AND ELLA HAD been telling the king and queen all about their adventure when they heard a familiar whooshing noise. They all turned around to see Agondray and Akoya right behind them.

"You're safe," exclaimed Pappy as he walked up to them.

"Yes, my friend, and I'm glad to see you are all safe, too. Your majesties, it is good to see you," Agondray said as he lowered his head in front of the king and queen.

"We are glad you are both safe. Your friends have been very brave and so have you. What has happened to Zell?" the king asked.

Agondray told the king and queen everything that had happened since they had been captured—from Zell taking his amulet and ordering him to leave and Pappy's plan for the rescue, also the fact that Zell was no longer a threat to Gibiuss.

"What good news," said the king, "Now peace will hopefully be restored for good. Have all our friends been told the good news?"

"Yes, they should be returning to the city as we speak," replied Akoya. "Excellent. We must return to the city immediately. There is much to do and organise. We will need to arrange temporary shelters for our friends until we can start to rebuild the city properly.

Agondray, we must return to our home and your human friends must return to theirs," said the king.

"Yes, your majesty. We will return them to their world," said Agondray.

The king turned to Pappy, Nan and the two children and said, "Thank you so much for your help. I don't think we can ever repay you for your bravery in rescuing us. Once the city has been rebuilt you must come with Agondray to visit our beautiful home."

"We would very much like that," replied Pappy,

"I must ask you one favour," said the king, "We have managed to keep our world a secret from yours all this time. I would be forever grateful if we could keep it that way."

"We can promise that we will not breathe a word to anyone," said Pappy.

The king and queen bowed to the family and then left to return to their city.

"Climb on, then," said Agondray. "It's time to take you home."

As they flew back down to earth, the children thought about what had happened. They thought about how no one would ever believe a story about dragons, battles, a castle in the sky and the rescue of a king and queen from Cloud Land. It would certainly make a good story for school though.

Once again, they flew through the funny-shaped clouds and headed back down to earth. Agondray and Akoya didn't fly so fast this time, so everyone had a chance to look around as they got closer to the ground. The view was totally amazing: they could see fields and houses for miles and, in the distance, they could see the farm house.

As they flew over the farm they saw their parent's car and Jessie running around in the field.

"Oh, no!" said Ben. "How are we going to explain this one?"

"Don't worry; I think it's time they knew any way," said Pappy and, with that, Agondray and Akoya landed in front of the house, right by the car.

Ben turned to Pappy, "But you promised the king you wouldn't tell anyone."

"I don't think he would mind me telling your parents. They are family and they won't tell anyone—who would believe them!?"

Jessie stopped running, stared at the two dragons and started to growl and bark. She was not quite sure if she was brave enough to get any closer, so she stayed where she was.

The children's parents came from inside the cottage to see what all the fuss was about and froze in the doorway.

The children climbed down off the dragon and ran over to their parents, who were still frozen in the doorway.

"Mum, Dad, we have had the most amazing time with battles and fire and a castle in the sky and . . . Are you okay?" Ella asked her parents.

"H-h-how? Wh-wh-who? W-w-what? Battles? What on earth has been going on?" cried Dad.

Robert walked up to the children's parents and said, "I think it's time I told you my little secret."

"Little secret?" exclaimed Mum, still staring at the dragons, "I think I must be seeing things. You have two . . . what look like . . . dragons in your front garden and you call that a little secret?"

"It's a long story," replied Pappy.

"Ben, Ella, go and say goodbye to Agondray and Akoya. They need to go before anyone else sees them," said Nan, "Then we will all go inside and explain everything."

The children ran up to the dragons and gave them each a hug. "We will miss you," said Ella.

"Thank you for your help. We will come and visit next time you are here and take you back to the city so you can see what a beautiful place it is—we promise," said Agondray.

"We can't wait!" said Ben.

"We will keep an eye on you both. And don't forget, just because you can't see us doesn't mean we're not there," said Akoya.

The children turned and walked towards their parents, who were still frozen in the doorway, unable to say anything else.

"I think they are in shock," said Nan. "We had better get them inside."

Agondray turned to Pappy and said, "Thank you, old friend. We will always be in your debt. Just remember: we are always here if you need us."

"I am glad we were able to help and that it ended well. Make sure you come and see us soon. Both of you," said Pappy.

"We will," replied Akoya.

"I am sorry we cannot stay longer, but we must leave before we are seen. Take care, Robert. Come on Akoya, we must go home," said Agondray. And with that, they both took to the sky with a whoosh and were gone.

Pappy turned towards the house and thought to himself, "How on earth do I explain this one?" Before he could open the front door someone behind him said, "Robert, glad you're back." It was his neighbour who had been looking after the animals while they were away. "You won't believe the storm we had down here last night. My goodness! Not much rain, but the noise of the thunder and the lightning was unlike any I've seen or heard for a while. Anyway, just to let you know I checked on your animals last night—all okay, no damage . . . just a few frightened lambs. I saw your family was here, so that's why I came over—to tell them—but, as I said, you're back now, so that's fine." "Thank you for keeping an eye on things for me, we will catch up later in the week," said Pappy. "That's okay, Robert, you need to go and attend to your family. I'll see you during the week, then." The neighbour then stood for a moment, scratching his head and said, "Just seen the strangest thing in the sky. Looked a bit odd to me—could have sworn it was a dragon. I must be going a bit soft in my old age. I think I'll phone Burt down the way to see if he saw anything. Could be one of those—you know—what's it called? Oh, I know, UFO things. Anyway, I'd best be off." And with that, Pappy's neighbour headed off towards the lane before Pappy got the chance to say anything.

"Oh, no! I think we might have a problem. Well, I can't do anything about that now; I will go and see him later and try to convince him it was just the shape of the clouds or something else. Besides, he may have forgotten about it by the time he gets home," Pappy thought to himself. "Right now, I need to speak to the family."

He walked into the house, sat down with the rest of the family, and said, "Right. I suppose I had better start at the beginning."

The End

ABOUT THE AUTHOR

Donna Goddard was born in Bristol and now lives in the sea
side town of Weston-super-Mare. She is married and has
two children, Ben and Ella. Agondray: The Guardian of the
Clouds is her first children's book. She loved fantasy books
as a child and then reading them to her own children. For
this story, she took inspiration from a long car journey while
playing look-at-the-shapes-in-the-clouds with her two young
children. She intends to write many more books—with the
next one being a sequel to the first.